WHAT DO YOU SAY?

By Jennifer B. Gillis
Illustrated by Ann Iosa

Table of Contents

Illustrations on pages 20–23 created by Carol Stutz

All inquiries should be addressed to:
Barron's Educational Series, Inc.
250 Wireless Boulevard
Hauppauge, New York 11788
www.barronseduc.com

Library of Congress Catalog Card No.: 2005054189

ISBN-13: 978-0-7641-3298-8
ISBN-10: 0-7641-3298-9

Library of Congress Cataloging-in-Publication Data
Gillis, Jennifer Blizin, 1950–
        What do you say? / Jennifer B. Gillis.
            p. cm. – (Reader's clubhouse)
        Summary: Prompted by her mother, Eve displays her good manners while playing in the park. Includes facts about good manners, a related activity, and word list.
            ISBN-13: 978-0-7641-3298-8
            ISBN-10: 0-7641-3298-9
            (1. Etiquette—Fiction. 2. Behavior—Fiction. 3. Mothers and daughters—Fiction. 4. Play—Fiction.) I. Title. II. Series.

PZ7.G4156Wh 2006
(E)—dc22

                                                                            2005054189

PRINTED IN CHINA
9 8 7 6 5 4 3 2

Dear Parent and Educator,

Welcome to the Barron's Reader's Clubhouse, a series of books that provide a phonics approach to reading.

Phonics is the relationship between letters and sounds. It is a system that teaches children that letters have specific sounds. Level 1 books introduce the short-vowel sounds. Level 2 books progress to the long-vowel sounds. This progression matches how phonics is taught in many classrooms.

What Do You Say? reviews the long "a" and "e" sounds introduced in previous Level 2 books. Simple words with these long-vowel sounds are called **decodable words.** The child knows how to sound out these words because he or she has learned the sounds they include. This story also contains **high-frequency words.** These are common, everyday words that the child learns to read by sight. High-frequency words help ensure fluency and comprehension. **Challenging words** go a little beyond the reading level. The child will identify these words with help from the illustration on the page. All words are listed by their category on page 24.

Here are some coaching and prompting statements you can use to help a young reader read *What Do You Say?:*

- **On page 4, "Eve" is a decodable word. Point to the word and say:**

  Read this word. How did you know the word? What sounds did it make?

  Note: There are many opportunities to repeat the above instruction throughout the book.

- **On page 4, "seesaw" is a challenging word. Cover the word *saw* and say:**

  Read this part of the word. (Then cover the word *see* and say:) *Read this part of the word.* (Then point to the whole word and say:) *Read this word. How did you know the word? Did you look at the picture? How did it help?*

You'll find more coaching ideas on the Reader's Clubhouse Web site: *www.barronsclubhouse.com.* Reader's Clubhouse is designed to teach and reinforce reading skills in a fun way. We hope you enjoy helping children discover their love of reading!

Sincerely,

Nancy Harris

Nancy Harris
Reading Consultant

"I want to ride the seesaw," says Eve. "What do you say?" Mom asks.

"**Please** may I ride?"
asks Eve. "Yes," say
Reece and Jade.

"I want to play that game,"
says Eve. "What do you
say?" Mom asks.

"Please may I play?"
asks Eve. "Yes," say Nate
and Jake.

"I want to feed the geese,"
says Eve. "What do you
say?" Mom asks.

"Please may I feed the geese?" asks Eve. "Yes," says Mr. Neal.

"I want to rake, too," says Eve. "What do you say?" asks Mom.

"Please may I rake?" asks
Eve. "Yes," says Ms. Dean.

"I want to paint," says
Eve. "What do you say?"
Mom asks.

"Please may I paint?" asks
Eve. "No," says the man.
"I cannot let you paint."

"I want to walk the dog,"
says Eve. "What do you
say?" Mom asks.

"Please may I walk the dog?" asks Eve. "Yes, you may," says Steve.

"Oh, no! The leash!"
says Steve.
"Help!" screams Eve.

"Stop!" yells Steve.

"What do we say?" asks Eve.
"Thank you," says Steve.

"You are welcome,"
says Ms. Dean.

Fun Facts About
Manners

It is always polite to say "please" and "thank you," but words are not the only tools we can use to express good manners. Our faces, feet, and hands can also express manners, both good and bad.

If you travel to other countries, the way you use your body can send different messages.

- In India, people's feet and shoes are thought to be dirty. If your foot or shoe touches another person, you should say you're sorry.

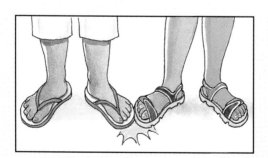

- To a religious family in Thailand, it is offensive to touch a child's head. The head is considered to be the soul of Buddha, who is the most important person in their religion.

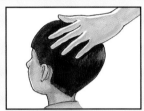

- In Thai and Japanese cultures it is rude to look someone straight in the eye because it is seen as showing a lack of respect.

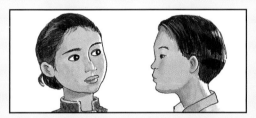

- In the United States, this means "O.K." In Japan, it means "money." In France, it means "zero."

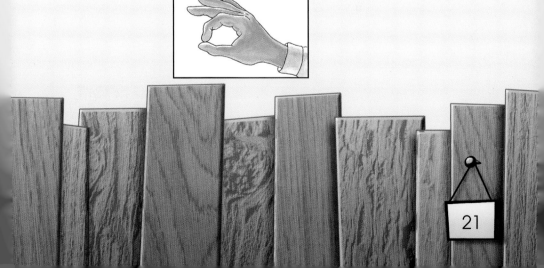

Mother, May I?

Yes, you may if you say "please" and "Thank you!"

In this version of an old game, players have to use good manners to move forward.

- Players choose one person to be the mother. The mother does not have to be a girl.

- The mother stands in front of all the other players, who are lined up in a row.

- Players take turns asking mother if they may move forward. They must use the word "please" when they ask. After mother gives them permission, they must say "thank you." If a player does not say "please" or "thank you," mother may send them backward.

- The first person to reach the mother becomes the new mother. The game continues . . . .

Word List

Challenging Words	Mr.	seesaw
	Ms.	welcome

Long A-E Decodable Words	Dean	Nate
	Eve	Neal
	feed	paint
	game	rake
	geese	Reece
	Jade	screams
	Jake	Steve
	leash	

High-Frequency Words	and	stop
	are	thank
	asks	that
	do	the
	help	to
	I	too
	let	walk
	may	want
	no	we
	oh	what
	play	you
	please	
	say	
	says	